The Missing
Necklace

by Katie Dale and Ben Scruton

W
FRANKLIN WATTS
LONDON•SYDNEY

A very long time ago in Egypt, Ana went to the well for a cool drink of water. As she was collecting some water, a magpie flew down from its nest. "You must be thirsty too," Ana said, pouring it some water.

Then she took a drink to her father,

who was the chief palace guard.

"Thank you, Ana," he smiled.

Suddenly, they heard a loud scream.

"That's the Queen!" Ana's father cried.

They found the Queen in her bedroom
with her bodyguard, Sabaf, and her maid, Tem.
"My necklace is missing!" the Queen wailed.
"Only Tem and I have been inside
the Queen's bedroom today," Sabaf said.
"So Tem must have taken it!"

"I didn't take it!" Tem cried. "I saw the Queen
leave her necklace by the open window.
Bek the gardener could have taken it!"

"Bek!" Ana's father shouted. "Did you take the Queen's necklace?"

Bek was shocked. "No, of course not!" he replied, hurrying over.

Tem said, "I heard Bek moaning that he doesn't earn enough money, but he had a plan to get more. I think he meant he was going to sell the necklace!"

"I wasn't!" Bek cried. "I just meant that I was going to work harder to earn more money! But the window was open all day. I heard the Queen shouting at Tem. She told her to leave the palace at once."

Ana felt sorry for Bek.

Then Ana's father turned to Tem.

"Is this true? Did you lose your job?"

Tem nodded miserably. "I spilt wine on
the Queen's favourite dress and she was furious.

Now Ana felt sorry for Tem.

"But I didn't steal her necklace!" Tem insisted.

"I've never stolen anything in my life,
but Sabaf has!"

"Sabaf stole leftover bread from the Queen's breakfast this morning," Tem said.

"I was going to tell the Queen,

but he promised he'd never do it again.

Once a thief, always a thief."

Ana's father turned to Sabaf. "Is this true?

Did you steal the bread?"

"I did take it," Sabaf admitted. "I threw
some breadcrumbs to the magpies.
The bread was going to be thrown away,
so it didn't seem like stealing.
I'd never take anything valuable!"
Now Ana felt sorry for Sabaf.

Ana's father looked at Tem, Sabaf and Bek.
"You three were the only people who could
have stolen the Queen's necklace," he said.
"Whoever took it, confess now, or you will
all be punished!"

Tem trembled, and Bek and Sabaf looked at each other, but no one spoke.

Ana watched them nervously. Who was the thief? She did not want to believe any of them had stolen the necklace.

"Since none of you will confess, I have no choice but to punish you all!" said Ana's father.

"Wait!" cried Ana. She had an idea.

"Tem, you said the Queen left her necklace by the window," said Ana. Tem nodded.

"Bek, you said the Queen left her window open all day," Ana continued. Bek nodded.

"And Sabaf, you said you threw

breadcrumbs to the magpies from her room.

I think I know where the necklace is.

Quick, follow me!" she cried.

They all hurried after Ana.

"There's the thief!" Ana pointed up

at the tree where a magpie sat by a nest.

There, shining brightly, was the necklace!

Everyone gasped.

"How did you know it would be there?"

asked Ana's father.

"Magpies love to steal anything shiny,"

laughed Ana. "Sabaf's crumbs led them

straight through the open window

to the Queen's necklace!"

Sabaf looked at Tem. "I was wrong," he said. "You didn't take it. I should not have said so before I had proof. I'm sorry."

"I'm sorry too," said Bek to Tem.

"And so am I," Tem said to Bek and Sabaf.

Together, they got the Queen's necklace back.

Bek, Tem and Sabaf told the Queen that Ana had found the missing necklace.

"Thank you so much!" the Queen said to Ana.

"How can I ever repay you?"

Ana whispered in the Queen's ear.

The Queen smiled. She started paying Bek more money and gave Tem her job back. She also gave Sabaf lots of bread to feed the birds. Everyone was happy, except the magpie who stole the shiny necklace!

Story order

Look at these 5 pictures and captions.
Put the pictures in the right order
to retell the story.

1

Ana knows where to find the necklace.

2

Everyone is happy, except the magpie.

3

Tem the gardner is not to blame.

4

No one owns up to the theft.

5

The Queen's necklace has gone missing.

Independent Reading

This series is designed to provide an opportunity for your child to read on their own. These notes are written for you to help your child choose a book and to read it independently.

In school, your child's teacher will often be using reading books which have been banded to support the process of learning to read. Use the book band colour your child is reading in school to help you make a good choice. *The Missing Necklace* is a good choice for children reading at White Band in their classroom to read independently.

The aim of independent reading is to read this book with ease, so that your child enjoys the story and relates it to their own experiences.

About the book

Ana and her father rush to help the Queen when her precious necklace goes missing. There only seems to be three possible culprits: Tem, the maid, Bek, the gardner and Sabaf, the Queen's bodyguard. But all protest their innocence. Perhaps there is another thief?

Before reading

Help your child to learn how to make good choices by asking:
"Why did you choose this book? Why do you think you will enjoy it?"
Look at the cover together and ask: "What sort of story do you think this will be? Is there a puzzle to solve? What do you know about puzzle or detective stories?" You could also discuss the particular historical setting indicated by the cover. Remind your child that they can sound out letters or groups of syllables to make a word if they get stuck.

Decide together whether your child will read the story independently or read it aloud to you.

During reading

Remind your child of what they know and what they can do independently. If reading aloud, support your child if they hesitate or ask for help by telling the word. If reading to themselves, remind your child that they can come and ask for your help if stuck.

After reading

Support comprehension by asking your child to tell you about the story. Use the story order puzzle to encourage your child to retell the story in the right sequence, in their own words. The correct sequence can be found on the next page.

Help your child think about the messages in the book that go beyond the story and ask: "Why did each character blame another person for the theft?" Do you think it is good to blame people if you are not sure about something? How important is it to listen to all points of view before making a decision?"

Give your child a chance to respond to the story: "How did each character feel when they were blamed for the theft? How would you feel if you were blamed for something you didn't do? What would you do about it?"

Extending learning

Help your child recognise some aspects of a puzzle story by identifying the key events in the plot. What clues can be found in the words and pictures to help establish the thief's true identity?

In the classroom, your child's teacher may be teaching about possessive apostrophes, such as "the Queen's necklace". Ask your child to look through the story for more examples and discuss how they help to shorten sentences.

Franklin Watts
First published in Great Britain in 2018
by The Watts Publishing Group

Series Editors: Jackie Hamley and Melanie Palmer
Series Advisors: Dr Sue Bodman and Glen Franklin
Series Designer: Peter Scoulding

A CIP catalogue record for this book is
available from the British Library.

ISBN 978 1 4451 6264 5 (hbk)
ISBN 978 1 4451 6266 9 (pbk)
ISBN 978 1 4451 6265 2 (library ebook)

Printed in China

Franklin Watts
An imprint of
Hachette Children's Group
Part of The Watts Publishing Group
Carmelite House
50 Victoria Embankment
London EC4Y 0DZ

An Hachette UK Company
www.hachette.co.uk

www.franklinwatts.co.uk

Answer to Story order: 5,3,4,1,2